#1 FAN BOOK

Written by
Jim Razzi

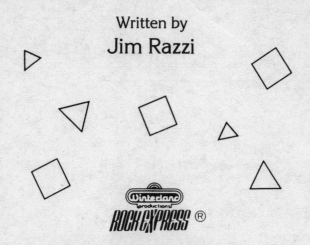

A GOLDEN BOOK · NEW YORK
Western Publishing Company, Inc., Racine, Wisconsin 53404

S0-BUA-679

Table of Contents

Introduction

You love thinking and dreaming about New Kids on the Block, right? Who doesn't? This is the book for you.

Start out with your New Kids diary, where you can record all your personal New Kids facts. Dream on with the New Kids dream diary. You'll find scrapbook pages for all your favorite New Kids things, pages that turn into letters, cards you can send to the Fab Five, a super-fun New Kids game, and more!

All you need to have a great time with this book is a good imagination. (A pen, a pencil, and lots of rad New Kids stuff will help, too.) Have a super time!

Did You Know That...

when Danny was fourteen, he fell off a fifty-foot cliff and narrowly escaped death?

Donnie has a superstition about shaving before going on stage? (He never does.)

Joe's favorite place to take a date is Disney World?

when the group was first formed, they were named NYNUK?

a fortune-teller foretold that a young girl would help make the New Kids famous? (She did. Her name is Tiffany.)

Jordan is a reformed graffiti pest?

Donnie would love to have a girlfriend and take her for walks on the beach?

the New Kids grew up around drugs and violence but were determined to do good things with their lives?

Jon is nicknamed GQ because he loves shopping for clothes?

Did You Know That...

New Kids on the Block got their name from one of their first rap tunes?

Joe misses going to a regular high school?

the first time the New Kids performed in public was at a prison in Massachusetts?

Donnie's first dream was to be a baseball star?

if Danny likes a girl, he gets so nervous he can hardly speak to her?

Joe's voice has gotten deeper since he first sang "Please Don't Go, Girl"? (Now he has to sing it in a lower key!)

the Kids' official fan club has more than one hundred thousand members?

Donnie's bedroom walls are covered with collages of all the fans who sent him pictures?

Dream Diary

Did you ever daydream about meeting one of the New Kids on the Block? Here's your chance to write in your Dream Diary about what might happen.

Dear Dream Diary:

I still can't believe what happened yesterday! I was standing outside the stage door of a New Kids concert when all of a sudden this boy bumped into me. I looked at him and said, "_____

_____."

The boy had a hat pushed down just above his eyes, but I would recognize Donnie anywhere! I immediately _____.

Donnie asked for my help. He had to get into the concert hall without being stopped by all his fans, or he would be late for the performance. I had an idea. I told Donnie I would make believe I _____

_____.

Well, my idea worked, and when Donnie and I were safely inside the hall, he looked into my eyes and

_____.

Dear Dream Diary:

Today my girlfriend and I went to a homeless shelter to help out. We were just leaving when who should walk in the door but adorable Joe! Talk about instant payoffs for good deeds!

My girlfriend and I turned around and _____

_____.

Joe told us he had great concern for the homeless and asked what we thought about it. I said, "_____

_____."

Joe gave me a sweet smile and answered, "I've been waiting a long time to meet a girl like you. Would

you _____

_____?"

My girlfriend had to hold me up before I fainted dead away. Imagine being with Joe and _____

_____!

It was a perfect day.

Dear Dream Diary:

I had finished doing my chores and was just about to listen to my "Hangin' Tough" album when the front doorbell rang.

When I answered the door, I couldn't believe my eyes! It was Danny!

He explained that the New Kids' tour bus had broken down and asked if he could make a call.

I said, "_____."

Danny came into the living room, and the first thing he did was _____

_____.

I didn't know what to do first, so I just _____

_____.

After Danny made the call, he asked me if I would like to _____.

I said, "Would I!" So Danny and I spent the rest of the afternoon _____

_____.

I had never had a more excellent time!

Dear Dream Diary:

Today I was walking in the rain, and my mood was as gloomy as the weather.

I was just turning a corner when a cute boy bumped right into me. I had almost snarled at him when I saw it was Jordan!

Jordan took one look at my face and asked what was wrong.

I told him what was bothering me. It was _____

_____

_____.

Jordan walked along with me.

"When things go wrong," he said, "you've got to hang tough and be positive about yourself. I'll bet you have a lot of good things happening in your life, too."

I looked at him and realized he was right. I started to talk about the good things. I told him about _____

_____

_____.

When I was finished talking, the sun had come out. I smiled at Jordan. And he gave me the most gorgeous smile back!

Dear Dream Diary:

I'll never forget this day as long as I live!

This morning I was riding my bike down Maple Street when a limo cut me off. I swerved aside just in time, but I lost my balance and fell.

The limo stopped, and who should get out of the back but Jon!

He helped me up and said, "_____

_____."

I was so tongue-tied, I couldn't say anything. But I did manage to _____

_____.

After that, Jon put my bike in back of the limo and told me that he was going to _____

_____.

He dropped me off right in front of my house, where a bunch of my friends were hanging out.

When they saw Jon, they screamed and _____

_____.

It was an amazing day!

Fab Five Fan Fun

It's fun! It's crazy! It's live!
It's the Fab Five Fan Game.
Here's how to start:

One player is selected to be the READER. The READER picks one of the stories on the following pages. The READER does not tell the other players which story he/she has selected.

How to play:

The READER will ask each of the players in turn to call out a word. The word will be whatever is called for underneath the blank space. The player should try to think of the wackiest words he/she can.

When all the blank spaces have been filled in, the READER reads the story aloud.

Note: A THING is any inanimate object like ROCK or PIANO. A PLACE is any location like BATHROOM, CELLAR, STREET, or PARK. A MOOD is any feeling like SILLY, HAPPY, or CRAZY.

All other words are self-explanatory. (The READER should pencil in all the words lightly for repeat plays.)

Here's a sample game:

(*Before play*)

Joe gets up from the _____ on the tour
                          A THING

bus and looks _____. "Hey!" yells
                    A MOOD

Donnie. "Stop looking so _____.
                              A ROCK STAR

Let's play with our new _____." "Okay,"
                            AN ANIMAL

answers Joe, "but not in the _____
                                  A PLACE

like last time."

(*After play*)

Joe gets up from the *mushroom* on the tour
                      A THING

bus and looks *silly*. "Hey!" yells
                  A MOOD

Donnie. "Stop looking so *Madonna*.
                            A ROCK STAR

Let's play with our new *monkey*." "Okay,"
                          AN ANIMAL

answers Joe, "but not in the *bathroom*
                                A PLACE

like last time."

CLOSE ENCOUNTER

_____ is just in time to
PLAYER'S NAME (GIRL)

see Danny come out the _____ door.
A PLACE

He is wearing a hairy _____
ARTICLE OF CLOTHING

and a pair of muddy _____.
FOOTWEAR

When _____ sees him she
SAME PLAYER'S NAME

rushes into the _____ and asks him
A PLACE

for his _____. "I'll be glad to give you
A THING

my _____," says Danny as he smiles
A THING

and blows a _____ to
A THING

_____. _____
SAME PLAYER'S NAME   SAME PLAYER'S NAME

looks _____ and says, "Thank you,
A MOOD

you adorable _____!"
A THING

DREAM DATE

_____ is on a date with
  PLAYER'S NAME (GIRL)

Joe and is so excited she starts to act like

a _____.
      AN ANIMAL

Joe is wearing a furry _____
                ARTICLE OF CLOTHING

and she wears a purple and green

_____.
  ARTICLE OF CLOTHING

They go to a _____ first, and then
              A PLACE

Joe takes her to see his _____.
                          A THING

When _____ sees that, she
    SAME PLAYER'S NAME

looks _____ and starts to
        A MOOD

_____.
  AN ACTION

Later on, Joe gives her a big _____
                              A THING

to remember him by.

THE TRYOUT

_____ gets a call from Jordan.
PLAYER'S NAME (BOY)

His brother Jon can't perform that night and they

need a replacement. Jordan asks

_____ what _____
SAME PLAYER'S NAME   *A THING*

he plays best. "The _____!"
             A THING

_____ says.
SAME PLAYER'S NAME

"Can you act _____?" asks Jordan.
        A MOOD

"Sure thing," _____ answers,
       SAME PLAYER'S NAME

"and I can even imitate a _____ on
         AN ANIMAL

stage. "Rad," says Jordan. "But can you imitate

_____ on stage?"
A ROCK STAR

"Sure thing," _____ answers.
       SAME PLAYER'S NAME

"But I have to do it with a _____."
          A THING

"You've got the job," says Jordan.

THE INTERVIEW

_____ gets an exclusive interview
PLAYER'S NAME (GIRL)

with Donnie. The dreamy-looking heartthrob looks

cute wearing a _____ on his head.
                              A THING

But _____ gets right down to
       SAME PLAYER'S NAME

business. "What do you like in a girl?" she asks.

"She has to look like a _____
                                    AN ANIMAL

and act like _____ all the time,"
                    A ROCK STAR

Donnie answers. "I also like her to have a

_____ just like you."
       A BODY PART

_____ blushes like a
   SAME PLAYER'S NAME

_____ and drops her
       A FRUIT

_____. "Thanks for the interview,"
       A THING

_____ says. "It'll be great for
   SAME PLAYER'S NAME

our school _____." "It's a pleasure
                    A PLACE

giving an interview to such a sweet

_____," Donnie answers.
       A FRUIT

17

NEW SONG

The Kids have just composed a tender new love

song called "Lying Eyes" and here are the lyrics.

"You told me you loved my _____ and

A THING

I believed you. But I didn't know you were lying

through your _____.

PART OF FACE

So now I'm left alone with only the memory of your

pretty _____ face and the way we used

A COLOR

to run through the _____ with

A PLACE

flowers in our _____.

PART OF FACE - PLURAL

I shouldn't have gazed into your lying eyes or

listened to your tender sighs.

So now I have a _____ in my ear,

A FRUIT

No longer your lying words to hear.

And I've put a _____ over my eyes,

A THING

No longer to see your lies."

STUCK WITH THE KIDS

_____ gets on an elevator at the
PLAYER'S NAME (GIRL)
hotel she's staying at. There are five other riders—

the New Kids on the Block! They are each wearing

a _____ in their ear.
      A THING
And sporting a haircut like _____.
                            A ROCK STAR
The Kids smile and say, "What _____
                              A PLACE
are you getting off at?" _____
                         SAME PLAYER'S NAME
nervously pushes the wrong _____
                           A THING
and the elevator gets stuck between floors! Jordan

smiles and says, "It's a _____
                         A MOOD
situation." _____ sighs and
            SAME PLAYER'S NAME
thinks, "It's a _____ situation
                A MOOD
as far as I'm concerned!"

ON STAGE

The New Kids on the Block run onto the stage

holding a _____ in their hands. The
A THING

fans squeal in glee as Danny jumps up on a

_____ and does a split.
AN ANIMAL

In turn, each of the other Kids puts a

_____ on his _____
ARTICLE OF CLOTHING   PART OF BODY

and dances around the _____. At
A THING

that point Joe grabs a _____ and
A THING

starts to sing into it. The fans go wild and throw

_____ at the New Kids. The New Kids
FRUIT - PLURAL

laugh and throw _____ back. The
FRUIT - PLURAL

fans cheer and clap as the New Kids take a bow

and head for the _____.
A PLACE

ON THE STREET

The New Kids are trying to walk around town

without being recognized. They are each wearing

a _____ over their eyes and a
    A FRUIT

_____ on their feet. But their fans see
    A THING

through their disguises and the New Kids have to

dash into a nearby _____ to escape.
                        A PLACE

They just start to relax, when they realize they are

trapped by a huge _____ that looks
                        AN ANIMAL

like _____. Jon is about to run for
    ANY PLAYER'S NAME

help when a lady corners him and starts to rip

the _____ off his back. "I just love the
    A THING

New Kids!" she screams as she squeezes Jon's

_____ in glee. The New Kids sigh. It's
    PART OF BODY

just another typical outing!

Meeting the New Kids On The Block
My Most Embarrassing Moment

Lots of kids would do anything to meet the New Kids—at least, that's what they think! Here's the story of what happened to one girl who wanted to make her dream come true. What would you do?

Two weeks ago the New Kids came to town to give a benefit concert for the local hospital. So, of course, I and a million other fans mobbed the theater where the concert was being held.

I had always dreamed of meeting the New Kids face-to-face. But, like a lot of other girls, I knew that it was almost an impossible dream.

Anyway, I kept on dreaming, and two weeks ago my dream came true. But it didn't start out like a dream. It started out like a nightmare!

I should also tell you that I like to write stories and am always making up things in my head. My friends say I have a real talent for it.

Well, let me tell you that having a talent can sometimes also be a curse. And the reason I know that is because of what happened that day.

I was standing outside of the theater where the New Kids were playing, when all of a sudden this long black limo pulls up, and who should get out but the Fab Five!

Everybody started to scream and push, and before I knew it, I was caught up in a tidal wave of teenagers trying to meet the New Kids.

I don't know how it happened, but all of a sudden I found myself right at the stage door where the New Kids had just gone in.

There was a gray-haired man at the door, and for a second, he looked as if he were going to hold the door open for me.

On the spur of the moment, I had this wild inspiration.

I smiled at the man and said, "I'm one of Joe's sisters," and I started to squeeze past him.

I knew that Joe had a lot of sisters, so I figured that the man wouldn't really know any of them. I was right, because he hesitated for a second, but then he let me in.

I was wild with excitement as I followed the New Kids through a long hallway to their dressing room. There were a lot of people around, but no one noticed me.

My heart pounded in my chest as I found myself right in front of the Kids' dressing room. I was trying to figure out my next move, when all of a sudden this big guy came over and grabbed my arm. He was one of the Kids' bodyguards.

"Who are you, young lady?" he asked.

"Uh, I'm one of Joe's sisters," I blurted out, still sticking to my story.

"Yeah, well, I know all of Joe's sisters, and I don't think you're one of them," the bodyguard answered.

"Uh, yes I am," I continued, thinking fast. "I've just been out of the country for a long time."

The bodyguard raised his eyebrows.

I didn't know what else to do but continue.

"I was placed with foster parents in South America," I quickly went on. "You know, when I was born it was just too many kids, and my mother and father just couldn't take one more."

I knew my face was getting red, but now that I had started, I didn't know how to get out of it.

"South America, eh?" the bodyguard said.

I nodded my head, like one of those dolls at the back of a car.

"That's right," I answered. "And Joe hasn't seen me in four years. My folks just happened to be in town for a banana convention, and…"

Too late, I realized that I had been shouting, and the bodyguard started to escort me away.

"I think you'd better leave," he said.

By this time, people were looking, and I felt my face go as red as a beet. To make matters worse, the dressing-room door opened and the New Kids came out to see what the commotion was.

Joe was the last one out, and when he heard the bodyguard repeat what I had been saying, he came over and gave me a dazzling smile and looked at me with those baby-blue eyes. I put my head down and looked at my feet. I was so embarrassed.

But suddenly, Joe yelled, "Sis! Is that you? I didn't recognize you, you've grown so much since I last saw you."

The bodyguard and the rest of the Kids looked on with wide eyes.

I stared at Joe, not knowing what was coming next. But he just kept smiling at me, and then he turned to the bodyguard and said, "It's okay."

Joe led me a little away from the group. Then he laughed out loud.

"What a story!" he said. "I just figured that anyone who could tell a tall tale like that is my kind of girl."

Then he looked serious.

"But you shouldn't lie. It only gets you into bigger and bigger trouble."

"Too right!" I said with a sigh.

I turned and started to go.

"Hey, hold on a second," Joe said. "As long as you're here, I'll introduce you to the rest of the gang."

For a moment he looked serious again.

"But only if you promise not to make up phony

stories anymore."

"Oh, I do! I do!" I cried.

Then I just couldn't help myself. I gave Joe a big hug and planted a kiss on his cheek.

"Oh, I love you, Joe, and that's the truth!" I said.

It was his turn to blush as he took my hand and led me toward the rest of the New Kids.

My New Kids On The Block Personal Diary

A diary is a book where you write down your most intimate thoughts. And here is your very own personal diary for your very own personal thoughts about the New Kids.

Dear New Kids On The Block Diary:

The first time I heard the New Kids, I was at _____

_____

_____.

I thought, "_____

_____."

At my first New Kids concert, I _____

_____

_____

_____.

The best part was when _____

_____

_____.

I would do almost anything to meet the New Kids face-to-face. I would even _____

_____

_____

_____.

If I could have *anything* I wanted from the New Kids, I would want _____

_____

_____

_____.

The reason I want this is _____

_____

_____.

I think Danny is absolutely_____

_____

_____

_____

_____.

On the other hand, Joe is _____

_____

_____

_____

_____

_____.

What thrills me most about Donnie is _____

_____

_____

_____

_____.

I love Jon. He's _____

_____

_____

_____

_____

_____.

But Jordan is just _____

_____

_____

_____

_____

_____ .

The New Kid I would most like to have a date with is

_____ , because_____

_____

_____

_____

_____

_____ .

When I listen to the New Kids, I feel _____

_____

_____

_____

_____ .

If I could have only ten minutes alone with one of the

New Kids, I would _____

_____.

Then I would _____

_____.

The New Kids have changed my attitude toward life.

Now I know that _____

_____

_____

_____

_____

_____.

If one of the Kids got married, I would _____

_____

_____

_____

_____

_____.

Precious Photos

You love looking at pictures of the New Kids, right? Now you can look at pictures of them and you, together! Just cut out a picture of one of the New Kids from a magazine and tape it next to a rad picture of yourself in one of the "frames" below. See what a perfect couple you make! Remember, the captions are New Kids songs, so choose your pictures carefully. You'll want the two of you to look totally awesome together.

Danny

You

"Be My Girl"

The Fab Five's famous smiles.

Donnie relaxes before a concert.

Danny, thinking about the girl of his dreams.

Jon wants to go horseback riding with you.

Gorgeous Jordan is ready to go for a ride with the top down.

Joe's "baby blues" are looking for you.

Jordan and Donnie take center stage.

New Kids on the Block (left to right) Jordan Knight, Jon Knight, Donnie Wahlberg, Danny Wood, and Joe McIntyre.

You　　　Jon

"Please Don't Go, Girl"

Jordan

You

"You Got It (The Right Stuff)"

Joe

TEEN MAG

You

"Cover Girl"

You

New
Kids
on the
Block

"Angel"

New Kids On The Block Scrapbook

Don't you just love saving anything and everything that has to do with the New Kids?

Well, here's your very own scrapbook where you can save those precious keepsakes forever!

Concert Tickets

Start by saving all your concert tickets and taping them in the spaces provided.

My very first New Kids concert ticket.
I remember _____

_____

_____.

My most exciting New Kids concert. I
had the best time when _____
_____
_____ .

My latest New Kids concert. When
they come to town again, I will_____
_____
_____ .

My favorite New Kids concert. It was
so cool that _____
_____
_____ .

Special Souvenirs

How about all those neat little things that bring back precious memories?

Here are some pages for buttons, decals, bubble-gum cards, photos, and anything else you can lay your lucky hands on.

(Tape or glue items in place.)

My Cool
Decals

The Cards I Cherish

**Funky
Photos**

Autographs

Wouldn't it be great to get autographs from the Fab Five? Well, just in case you ever get near enough to the New Kids, be prepared. Clip your favorite photos of each of the guys and paste them in the spaces provided. Then make sure you have a pen or pencil handy so they can autograph their fab photos for you.

Jon

Donnie

44

Joe

Jordan

Danny

New Kids on the Block

Articles About New Kids On The Block

How about all those articles about the Fab Five in the teen mags? Why not clip out your favorites so that you can read them again and again.

To put them in your scrapbook, tape the top edge of the clipping to the page and fold the sides and bottom to fit.

Here's What They Say About Donnie

My Favorite Story About Jon

A Super Cool Article About Joe

Catch All The Scoop About Donnie

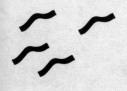

Everything You Wanted To Know About Jordan

Letter From The New Kids

*An excellent day! The New Kids have answered
your letter. You've got to save the reply!*

*Tape the top part of the letter to the page and
fold the sides and bottom to fit.*

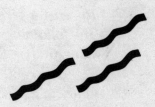

Send A Birthday Card To The New Kids

It's one of the New Kids' birthdays, and you've got to send him a card. You're in luck! There's a special card with a super message for each New Kid right on the following pages. To make your truly cool card, just cut along the dotted line of the card, then fold the card in half along the solid line. Sign it, send it, and just think of how excited your favorite New Kid will be to receive it!

To send a birthday card to one of the Fab Five, use the following address:
New Kids on the Block
P.O. Box 7080
Quincy, Massachusetts 02269

DANNY **JORDAN**

Jordan's birthday is May 17.
Joe's birthday is December 31.
Jon's birthday is November 29.
Danny's birthday is May 14.
Donnie's birthday is August 17.

JOE

JON **DONNIE**

(cut along dotted line)

Now's the time...
To act your age...

55

'Cause if you don't,
You'll burn the stage!!!

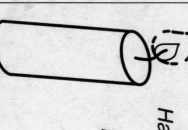

Happy Birthday, Jordan,
From Your
B-I-G-G-E-S-T Fan!

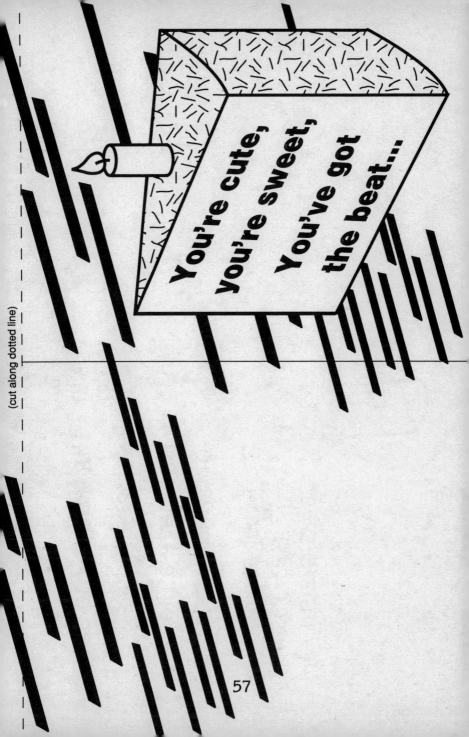

But today's the day

to take a break,

And have a piece

of birthday cake.

Happy Birthday, Joe,

From Your

B-I-G-G-E-S-T Fan!

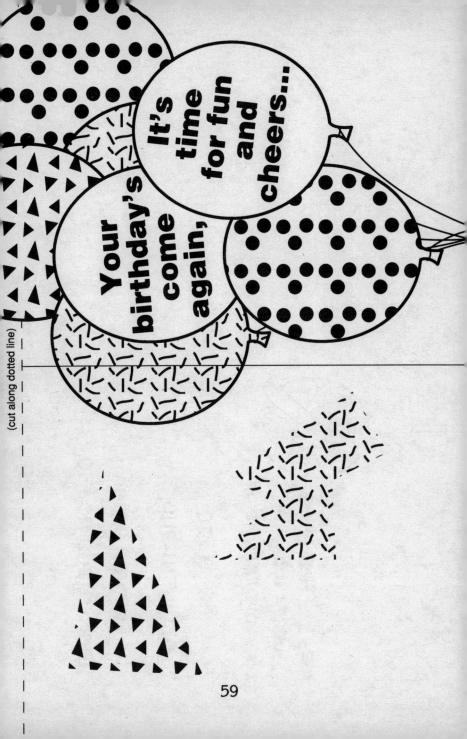

(cut along dotted line)

59

For you spend your
years so well,

Making music to
our ears!

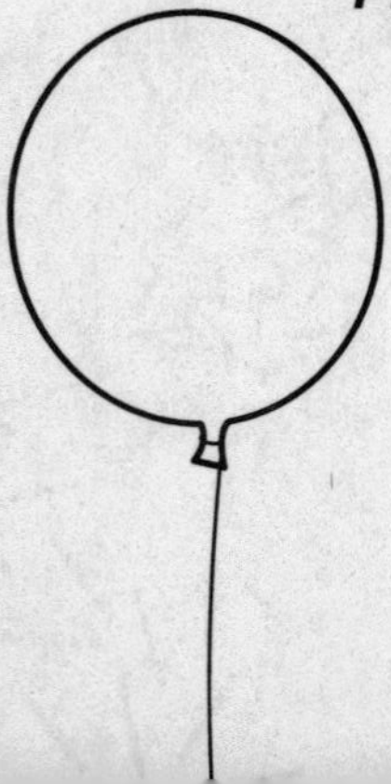

Happy Birthday, Donnie,
From Your
B-I-G-G-E-S-T Fan!

(cut along dotted line)

DEAR DANNY

You're my type of guy,
sweet as pie
and kind of shy...

It's up to me to
shout hurray,

And scream out loud
that it's your day!

Happy Birthday, Danny,
From Your
B-I-G-G-E-S-T Fan!

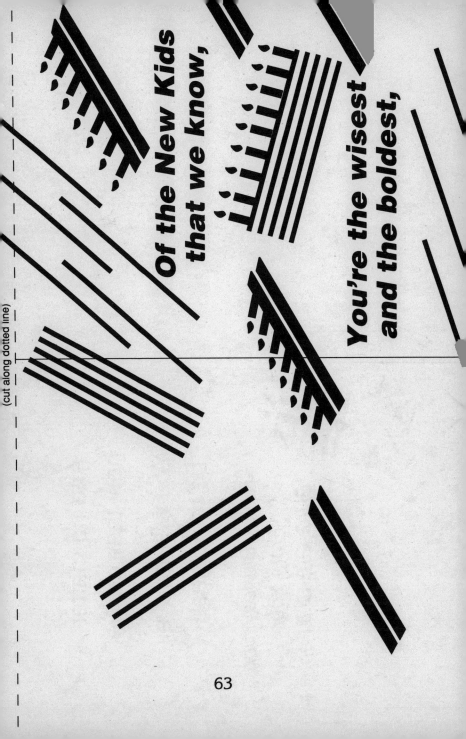

And no matter
how they grow,
You will always
be the oldest!

Happy Birthday, Jon,
From Your
B-I-G-G-E-S-T Fan!